FOUR SUITS

FOUR SUITS

A DECK OF 100-WORD STORIES

RAN WALKER

CONTENTS

In loving memory of Po'Teela

Curiouser and curiouser!

— LEWIS CARROLL, *ALICE'S ADVENTURES IN WONDERLAND*

PREFACE
(IN 100 WORDS)

My grandfather taught me how to play cards when I was quite young. I have since come to understand this was his preferred way of communicating with his grandchildren.

There are many life lessons he taught me through those games: teamwork, tenacity, patience, integrity, and magnanimity. Since then, I have been fascinated with cards, the look and feel of them.

In recent years, I have taken to collecting various card decks, and this collecting is what led me to wonder if I could write a collection representing every card in a deck.

It turns out I could.

This is it.

PART ONE
HEARTS

A 

The Tin Man was made to believe he could love without a heart, but Jameis has a problem with this. The word "heartless" by its very definition means that one is acting from a place quite opposite that of love. So why is the Tin Man not instinctively cruel? Maybe the cruelty is letting him believe he can love, or maybe he wants to challenge his true nature. Jameis can understand the desire to do this, but can one really get away from what they truly are? The way he sees it, there are things far worse than being heartless.

2 ♥

Usually, she would usher him out after they made love, but she sensed the time had come for him to share her bed overnight. She worried, though, that he might snore too loudly or that he might drool on her pillowcases or even pass gas during the middle of the night. Her allowing him to stay the night was a test run, she reminded herself.

Pleasantly surprised, she slept peacefully through the night.

She woke the following morning to his wide, Cheshire smile. She'd soon learn that she'd done everything she feared *he'd* do, although he didn't seem to mind.

3 ♥

It is only after the third set of compressions that Latasha's heart begins to beat again.

"You scared us for a moment," her friend Tara says.

Latasha can hardly speak and only vaguely remembers her friends shocking her. It was a game, wasn't it? They had challenged themselves to see if there was an afterlife.

"So…what did you see?" Alex asks.

Finally able to open her mouth, Latasha whispers, "Nothing. I don't remember there being anything."

This silences the group. Latasha was the first to go, but now everyone else is having second thoughts.

Nothing has become far scarier.

4 ♥

After their father passed away, the four of them got together once a year on his birthday, as he would have wanted them to, to remember him and fortify their sibling bond. It never occurred to them that they could have met up more regularly, as the two who lived out of state were still within driving distance. Instead, they turned their father's birthday into a holiday and treated it as such.

They never celebrated their mother, from whom they'd been estranged much of their lives, and, ironically, they might've been estranged from each other, if not for their father.

5 ♥

He fell for her on the fifth day of fall. They were standing at a scenic overlook, just off the Interstate, their eyes cast upon the sunset, a light breeze cascading from the distant mountains across the plain to tickle their shoulders. She nestled in close to him, and though they'd never stood that close to each other before, this felt right. They were a long way from their hometown and a long way from the university they attended, their weekend luggage packed in the back of his sedan. And up until that moment, they'd just been friends, just friends.

6 ♥

He has six tattoos of hearts hidden on his body, each one in a different place. Secretly, he loves hearts, but it is difficult being a football player with hearts tattooed on your body, so he has them strategically hidden, the way one might hide an undesired blemish or a secret middle name disguised as an initial. He is afraid of what someone might say should they see a heart…and then another…and another. Hearts aren't unicorns, but to a football player, they may as well be. So his six hearts remain hidden, though each longs to be free.

7 ♥

The other villagers feared the labyrinth, but AJ did not.

AJ was not preternaturally gifted in solving puzzles or discerning natural cartography or divining the minutia of various topiary. They had only their intuition, their feeling that their heart would guide them along the path they should go, so when the time came for the villagers to send forth a representative to attempt to retrieve the Treasure of Limbinus, AJ emerged the choice.

But this story is not about whether AJ was successful. It is about the fact that AJ met their challenge unafraid, and therefore, victory was indeed assured.

8 ♥

Molanto carved the bovine heart into eight pieces, one for each of his band of soldiers. It was believed those raw pieces of muscle would imbue them with the courage necessary to go into battle against the undead.

Baritore poked at the piece on his plate, struggling to muster the appetite to indulge. Molonto, Zabrius, Evendore, Listorius, Evanimus, Xavierton, and Ted had no problem chewing, though. In fact, Ted chewed so long, Baritore feared the muscle would never be consumed.

The band's lips bloody with this sacrifice, Baritore began to accept that only seven of them would go into battle.

9 ♥

They had broken up and gotten back together nine times (so far). It now felt like a routine. He would argue with her over her spending, which was cultivated by his rewarding her with shopping sprees when he felt like celebrating something (which was often). She would complain about the fact he worked too much and was never around. The shopping sprees silenced the criticism of his work; sex silenced the criticism of her shopping; and when neither worked, they broke up, only to find themselves getting back together, vowing a greater understanding of the other—which restarted the cycle.

10 ♥

They stood face-to-face, their fingers intertwined, searching for words. He'd always hated the idea of goodbyes, and she understood this. There were always FaceTime, messaging apps, and phone calls, but a year apart, one of them in an entirely different country, made things more complicated than either of them preferred. The plan was to leave things open and see where they stood when she returned. In that moment he wanted only to kiss every inch of her body, just to have the taste of her on his tongue before she boarded her flight, but his memories would have to do.

He was 45 when he realized Joe Jackson was saying "Me, babe" on the chorus of "Steppin' Out." This was not surprising, though. He messed up many lyrics from songs released in the 80s, from Prince to Michael Jackson.

He thought the lyric was "Wee-bey," like the character from *The Wire*—which made absolutely no sense, not the least of which was because the show came out roughly two decades after the song. He then rationalized that "wee-bey" was a white man's exaggerated take on the Ebonic phrase "we be" (steppin' out) because of the dropped "g."

"Me, babe." Damn.

Even as they celebrated their twelfth anniversary, they playfully debated when they'd first made love. He said it was the morning after their third date. She claimed it had been the night before. Both swore the other was wrong and wondered how something so important managed to escape the possibility of being "shared history" between them.

"You know I still love you, right?" he'd offer as a truce, and she'd take it, smiling, still wondering how he could forget their first time.

He would wonder the same thing, but in the end, all that mattered was that they were together.

In the beginning, she'd made fun of the fact that he'd named his dog King. It was the kind of thing that guys did (so cliché really, when you think about it), where'd they'd name their dogs powerful names, like Zeus or Caesar.

Then King began to grow on her, the way he snuggled against her calves while they watched movies, how he would strut whenever it was her turn to walk him.

At times she wondered if she loved King because she loved his owner, or if it was the other way around.

She dared not answer that question.

PART TWO
SPADES

Back when he was growing up, people began putting up Christmas decorations on the 1st of December. You had twenty-five days to get in all the seasonal activities before you started gearing up for the beginning of the new year, when school restarted.

Now, as he and his family strolled through the mall, they found Halloween/fall decorations alongside Christmas decorations, trees already lined up (they even had Halloween trees).

When had the world gotten itself in a hurry?

He wondered if his kids' memories of the seasons would be blurred with visions of goblins dancing in their heads.

2 ♠

And then there were two.

The lonely leaves clung to their nearly bare branch, their grips gradually loosening. Thousands of their fellow leaves had already fallen to the ground, where many were trampled underfoot or blown into piles and packed into bags. Such a forgettable disposition likely awaited the two of them, too, so they held on desperately, against winds and rains, talking to each other, providing inspiration and encouragement.

"You are more than a leaf," one would say.

"And you are magnificent, too," replied the other.

One day the wind came for one, then the other.

And they drifted.

3 ♠

Little Sheena drew this year's tree using only three lines, then colored the inside with a forest green crayon. This would be their tree this year, this small cutout drawn on a sheet of notebook paper and taped to the wall, near a corner. The gifts would go beneath the picture: small bags of fruit and candy canes. And they would sing carols and spread the joy of the season as if somehow that illustrated tree were in a different state of wood, branches thick with needles adorned in lights, ornaments, and tinsel, with wrapped gifts piled high beneath it.

4 ♠

On their first date, they walk through the campus quad, red and golden brown leaves beneath their sneakers, and it reminds him of the scene from *Coming to America* when Prince Akeem has to walk on rose petals. He shares this with her, and she smiles.

"So we are royalty?" she asks in jest.

"But of course." He starts to add "my queen," but it is still a first date, and while he is digging her, he knows it is bad luck to get too far ahead of himself.

With the sun setting behind them, she reaches for his hand.

5 ♠

They meet at their usual soul lounge after work, order their usual drinks, share the week's events, and await the DJ to spin gold like Rumplestiltskin, nostalgia from block parties years earlier filling the room so that the present can hardly fit.

He plays song after song, and they dance non-stop, between drinks, treating the week as if it were in the rearview of a car steadily speeding away.

Next week, they will return to this spot, order their usual drinks, share the week's events, and wait for the DJ to make sense of everything in their lives once again.

6 ♠

Flay was the resident chef in the apartment, though he rarely cooked for his room-mates, unless they bought all of the ingredients and he could eat well himself. The word was that he seasoned everything with one of six ingredients, though he would never confirm or deny this.

His roommates took it a step farther and started writing down their guesses on the white board that was affixed with magnets to the side of the refrigerator.

Salt
Pepper
Seasoned Salt
Worcestershire Sauce
Hot Sauce
(Unknown)

They couldn't figure out the sixth ingredient, nor would Flay volunteer it—or anything else.

7 ♠

After Brad Pitt asked Morgan Freeman what was in the box, there was a moment when he looked like he would vomit, that same face of disgust from that viral video of the little girl eating one of her mommy's meals and smiling to suppress the nausea, the exact same feeling I got watching Andy Dufresne crawl through a sewage pipe and throw up and then keep crawling through that feces and vomit to get to freedom. That feeling—the one that stays with you well after the film is over.

That scene might've contained Brad Pitt's best acting ever.

8 ♠

S hanice's grandfather told her that her age was the square root of his own. This didn't make sense to her, though, as she had no idea of what a *square root* was. It wasn't something her teachers had mentioned in the third grade, but he looked at her as if she would surely know the answer.

She started to ask him to just tell her, but the way he looked at her suggested he thought she was smart, and that made her feel good—especially coming from him.

So even though she didn't understand it, she nodded like she did.

9 ♠

The team manager handed him a jersey with the number 9.

For a while he stared at it, wondering if he *felt* like a 9. He'd never played with a single digit before, and there was nothing in his life that seemed to connect him to the number.

Maybe he could trade with someone for something in the 80s or 90s.

Could he run touchdowns with a 9 on his chest and back? He had no choice but to do it.

He would make 9 legendary.

Even though 9 didn't mean anything yet, he planned to make it mean everything.

10 ♠

Where others might've listed things in threes, Egbert felt the need to list things in tens.

The first couple of times he did this, he caught his friends and family off guard.

"First," he would start. Then "Second." When he went well past three, most of them would stare at him completely dumbfounded. Honestly, they thought, who had the time to come up with ten points of enumeration? At a certain point, it became less of a list and more of a soliloquy.

Out of kindness they would give him three. Then they would politely tell him to shut up.

J ♠

Terry modeled all of his comedic acting after Jack Black. In fact, he marketed himself in the industry as the Black Jack Black, which, when he actually thought about it, had a sing-song sound to it, a kind of "Jack" sandwich. His friends called him BJB for short, especially when he did an air guitar solo and rocked his locs back and forth to the beat. Though he was a bit thinner than his idol, Terry dressed in loose clothing and did his best to nail the actor's overall energy.

Did Hollywood need a Black Jack Black? Probably not.

It was a nickname she gave herself: Queen. Growing up, she found her teachers wrestled to pronounce her name. Even Black teachers whispered to each other how *ghetto* her name was, wondering if her mother had just made a portmanteau of her favorite celebrity names. Graduation was the last straw, though. After the principal pretended to mess up her name, she told people to call her Queen.

Throughout college and graduate school, people knew her only as Queen, and for every snicker, every comment made in jest, every roll of the eye, the world was forced to recognize her royalty.

He never called himself the king of the musical genre, although he pioneered everything from the rhythmic stylings, chord sequences, and vocal inflections that came to characterize the entire movement. English bands borrowed generously from his creations, crediting him to fans who couldn't be bothered to learn of their influences. In fact, the fans would crown another person, a derivative act, the true king of that musical genre, all but writing him out of the history.

But he didn't ask to be called the king. He understood that title was fleeting. He was more than that.

He was the *architect*.

PART THREE
DIAMONDS

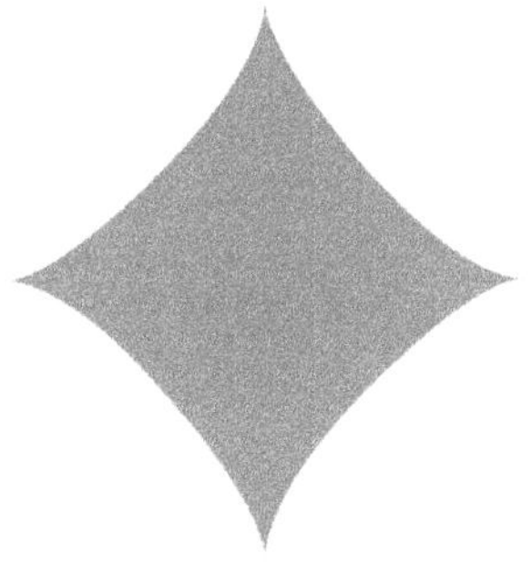

He broached the subject of engagement rings carefully, even though they had talked about getting married for the past three years. As it finally came time to purchase a ring and gather his ideas about proposing, he posed a casual question to her about what kind of carat and cut she might like.

A Marquise solitaire.

Two carats.

He didn't view himself as a Rhodes Scholar, but he knew immediately that the math didn't work out in his favor. He couldn't afford the ring she wanted, so he stopped talking about engagement.

They ultimately lived a quiet life together, unmarried.

2 ◆

He wore a gold grill with two diamonds on the top central incisors, so that he looked like a blinged-out rabbit when he opened his mouth. His rap name was a play off of carrots and carats, and he wanted to evoke the kind of facade that, when coupled with his gold-dyed locs and subtle facial tattoos, made him appeal to a wider base of fans.

He considered himself a better dancer than rapper, but his genre only required proof of star power.

He smiled in the mirror, his mouth glowing. He was now ready to take over the world.

3 ◆

Her grandmother referred to her jewels of wisdom as the three diamonds. They were as follows: don't do anything to embarrass yourself, don't do anything to embarrass your family, and don't do anything to embarrass the Black race. She wondered if non-Black children got the same talk as she, and if not, why her grandmother felt compelled to tell her this so frequently that she eventually found herself tangled in a thick web of respectability politics, always policing her actions so that some imaginary judge would quietly reward her for obeying these unwritten rules and deem her a good Negro.

4 ◆

Statistically, there were few hands that could beat four fours, especially when that last four came on a river and there were never three cards of a particular suit in the community cards. Throughout those three days, he'd played conservative at times, loose at others, even reckless a few times. Those who limped in calling on the flop were now out, and it was a head-to-head with one player, who was nearly impossible to read. That was the kind of hand you went all-in with in the final rounds of the World Series of Poker—so that's what he did.

5 ◆

They were different, yet the same, like cougars and mountain lions. They used different names for the same thing. He preferred *sofa*; she preferred *couch*. He drank soda; she drank pop. He rocked Air Force Ones; she rocked Uptowns. Even their names for each other differed: to him, they were exclusive; to her, he was her boyfriend.

They found this particular idiosyncrasy in their relationship amusing. Maybe they'd have a child one day whom he'd call Thomas but she'd call Tom. Or maybe they'd have five kids (which is what he'd say). Of course, she would say *a basket-ball team*.

6 ◆

Kareem's right hand was polydactyl, and when he was in school, the bullies had a field day with him, causing him to consider having the short, thin appendage surgically removed. His grandfather, one of his favorite people in the world, also had one, which is why he ultimately decided to keep it.

When he eventually became a famous actor—and those same bullies bragged about having gone to school with him as their primary claim to fame—he decided to buy diamond rings for each of his fingers, including the once derided and ridiculed sixth finger on his right hand.

7 ◆

The lights of the city shown through the blinds of his dormitory window illuminating her face. Her hands rested upon his bare chest, and his hands rested upon her hips, the heat of her body emanating through the thin fabric of her lingerie. The week had begun with them meeting for the first time at a record store and enjoying a conversation about the Soulquarians. Later, they would converse on the phone for hours, which led to their first date: lunch at a small bistro.

Until they kissed, they'd just been friends, but a lot could happen in seven days.

8 ◆

Carrie was born on August 8, 1988, weighing in at exactly eight pounds, and once she was old enough to understand numbers, she automatically gravitated toward the number 8, so much so that when she got older, she used it in the spellings of as many words as she could, wearing at the nerves of her English teachers, though her basketball and softball coaches knew what number to assign her, this woman who embodied the soul of a single number, in all of its gr8ness, and as f8 would have it, she planned to live to the age of 88.

9 ◆

The obituary the news stations put out after the passing of the movie star remarked about her lengthy filmography, highlighting three different Oscar nominations in three different decades (none of which she won), as well as the Lifetime Achievement Award the Academy eventually gave her as a consolation prize in the months before her death, brushing over more scandalous things like the shoplifting charges from Bloomingdale's and the DUI in Nevada—though those incidents didn't go completely ignored—settling on the odd, but well-known fact that she's been married nine times, three times to the same man, who predeceased her.

IO ◆

I t was never quite clear if the trustee assigned to post the Biblical Ten Commandments in the corridor of Red Clay County Courthouse was mistaken or actually pulled off a prank for the Culture. Instead of commandments carved into the tablets Moses carried down from Mount Sinai, the trustee, one Nathaniel "Young Nate" Townsend, instead posted a large poster of the Notorious B.I.G.'s "Ten Crack Commandments" from the classic *Life After Death* LP. The Honorable Jason Stegner considered putting Young Nate in contempt (if he could), but realized that was futile, given the trustee was still incarcerated.

N o one expected the author's book to be written on a single scroll of paper, its length so long it rolled from the editor's desk onto her chair, down onto the floor, through her door, running the length of the hall, then down the seven flights of stairs, out of those doors, past a security desk where one guard actually tried to read portions of it, across the expanse of the enormous lobby, through the revolving doors, onto the sidewalk, past a hotdog cart, an Italian ice stand, and two pizza shops, where it rolled steadily down the interminable road.

espite her best efforts to quell the fanatical loyalty of her many fans, they insisted on worshipping her. At first, they casually referred to her as "queen" (lowercase), not that different from a Hotep greeting, but over time "queen" morphed into "Queen." Then the tattoos started. It was only a matter of time before someone began accumulating all of her song lyrics (even those from the singing group she left) and fashioning them into a book that would eventually become a bible of sorts. Then the real worshipping began, and she found herself afraid of those who called to her.

K 

By the time he took the throne, his best years were behind him. His father had lived an extremely long life to the point many of the people in the country had forgotten the king had a son who would one day succeed him.

His ascension was largely unremarkable, as he struggled to keep an erect posture beneath the weight of medals and adornments he had not earned. His carriage traveled along roads named for his father, past buildings named for his father, home to his father's castle, as his constituents chanted, "The king is dead, long live the king!"

PART FOUR
CLUBS

In some distant multiverse, Michael Jeffrey Jordan works at a gas station in Wilmington, never having touched a basketball after being cut from his junior varsity team. While checking oil dipsticks, he is often asked if he played basketball, to which he shrugs and lowers the car hoods. The part of him that longed to compete has atrophied, leaving him with somber complacency.

When he gets off work, he will go home, crack open a beer, smoke a cigarette, and watch a baseball game with his father, his beaten Adidas sneakers resting on the tattered vinyl of his favorite recliner.

2 

The village sent the two of them to take down the beast haunting the forest. Both were sixteen, and while proficient with their weapons, they were far from the best warriors the village had to offer.

The truth was the village didn't know what they were dealing with, so they sent the two like armed scouts to test the vulnerabilities of the beast. They may as well have been sacrifices, expendable for the greater knowledge of those who would finish the job.

That is why villagers were surprised to see the blood-soaked teens enter the village, wielding the monster's head.

3 ♣

The little girl held three three-leaf clovers in the palm of her hand. They were a gift from the little boy next door. He'd said they were for good luck, so she'd taken them. She never asked his name, nor did he ask hers, but it was understood the two of them would be friends.

Her big sister told her that *four*-leaf clovers brought the most luck, so she vowed to look around her backyard for a four-leaf clover to give to the little boy. She wanted him to have good luck, as well—now that they had become friends.

The four suits mean many things to different people, so he treads lightly when he talks about them. He doesn't tell fortunes or give much regard to astrology. He is not even all that adept at the history of each shape or what the faces have come to represent. He is not a scholar of such things. Nor is he the type who can manipulate these pieces and fashion miracles for some and heartbreaks for others. He is merely an observer, a collector of beautiful things, and these suits are something he has come to believe he should be collecting.

There is something that lives under Andrea's bed. She has only really seen its glowing yellow eyes and its gnarled five fingers matted in dark fur with chipped nails, as if it crawled up through the house's foundation into the space beneath her boxspring. She is not afraid of this *thing*, which is why she doesn't refer to it as a monster. It is a *thing* until she is properly introduced to it. So she waits, only catching glimpse of eyes and fingers. Maybe it is afraid of her, she wonders, so she leaves cookies each night beside her slippers.

6 ♣

Percival spent the summer reading Percival Everett's books, hoping to get a glimpse of why his mother had named him after the writer. Unfortunately his mother had passed away years earlier, so he was left only with his imaginings of what she might have said, had he posed the question to her. Was there a presumed physical similarity, or had she read only his books while she was pregnant, hoping to boost his IQ as an infant? Maybe Percival was his mother's Mozart. He could only speculate at this point. And maybe that was the whole point of it all.

7 ♣

There was an air of irony as he contemplated whether to do the thing that was dangerous this week—while he was 27–versus next week when he would be 28. He knew there was a chance the thing would kill him, and he knew other's might see the need to place him in the 27 Club. This thing would not take him at 27–assuming it took him at all—but if it did get the better of him, 28 would be his age of departure, and in some small way that would make him different from the rest.

8 ♣

S he speaks only when spoken to, and even then she has little to say. Most questions posed to her require a single word of response.

"Are you hungry?"

"Did you finish your homework?"

She is content not to expend her vocabulary, no matter how robust it might be. That is the problem with most people, she reasons. They talk just to here themselves talk. Language should be used for communication, and sans the need to communicate, there is no need to speak. So she sits silently, reading and thinking but not speaking, less she dare pollute the air around her.

9 

Years before their relationship ended, they had carved the declarations of their love into nine different trees in the forest. This was something she had long forgotten until she went with her family to that forest last summer.

One of her children remarked that they kept finding her name carved into trees. In a wave, those moments from long ago returned to her, though she masked the undercurrent of emotions.

Her husband refused to inquire, though he could easily read her. He even nodded as she told the children that that was quite a spectacularly odd coincidence and nothing more.

10 ♣

"Ten toes down" is what the boy proclaimed through his immature bravado. He was prepared to fight, to defend his block against others who would cause harm to them. This is what was expected of him, this allegiance to others whose own existences were the very definition of meager. They would stand together to defend this land, this property that none of their families owned against others who were defending properties they, too, did not own, all because those before them had done the same. One day the property would house townhouses and Starbucks, but until then they would fight.

Back before Spike Lee merged the celebrations of Michael Jackson and Prince into a single block party, Raphael and Paris had met under a tent in Fort Green park. Each shy about speaking to the other, they found common ground in singing along with the music radiating across the grass.

Eventually the sun set upon them as the music of their own voices overtook J. Period's mixing of Michael's extensive catalog. While they grooved together, he took her hand, as one might a single white glove, and held it close to his chest, rejoicing in the curves of her lips.

Charlotte, the same girl who had been teased relentlessly by her two older brothers and all of her cousins, the one of whom the least had been expected by the entirety of her nuclear and extended families, was now the matriarch of the Randall family, five children and a bevy of grandchildren now regarding her as some kind of "ancient" queen with family and institutional knowledge and value to her community, but her true talent had been in surviving all of the others. Now, as she sat on her throne, it felt like any other chair she'd previously sat on.

K 

One day the seeds simply appeared beneath the callouses on his hands. Over time, the roots spread beneath his skin and across his palms, and eventually, one day saplings emerged from the split skin of both his hands. His tears mixed with the sunlight that bowed around the shadows that covered him and nourished those saplings until they became trees. From those burgeoning trees emerged branches covered in pages, then eventually books. And people read the fruit of his hands and rejoiced in this new knowledge. And he smiled, understanding now that his hands were the foundations of a library.

PART FIVE
JOKERS

BIG

When Heath jumps into the back of the bus, I am dumbstruck. The quickness. The unpredictability. The absurdity of it all. I am imagining Jack in the same scene. No. It doesn't work. I am imagining Joaquin in the same scene. It doesn't work. There is just something about Heath, the slight hunch of his shoulders, the movement of his tongue. You look into his eyes and it's clear the lights are out. The actors hold their collective breath, as do I. We know what *should* happen, but when Heath is on the screen we now understand anything is possible.

LITTLE

The laughter is like a whisper in the night air, and Lester can barely hear it. It is there, though. He senses it the way one might notice the hum of a refrigerator. It's almost staccato in its delivery, as if the person who is laughing must pause to catch a breath, then laugh again. Lester imagines that there is a tiny clown camped out under the canopy of a mushroom in the backyard, invisible to the world, so he must laugh to let others know that he is there. Otherwise, the world would not know that he even exists.

ACKNOWLEDGMENTS

Special thanks to Lauren and Zoë. I love you both beyond words.

I would also like to thank my family, my friends, and my readers, as well as the many writers of both short and long fiction who have inspired me throughout the years.

ABOUT THE AUTHOR
(IN 100 WORDS)

Ran Walker (he/him) is an award-winning author of over 30 books. His short stories, flash fiction, microfiction, and poetry have appeared in a variety of anthologies and journals. Prior to becoming a writer and educator, he worked in magazine publishing and practiced law in Mississippi. He is the creator of the 100 x 100 micro novel and serves as a contributing editor for *Writer's Digest*. He is an associate professor of creative writing at Hampton University and teaches with Writer's Digest University. He lives in Virginia with his wife and better half, Lauren, and his amazing daughter, Zoë.

ALSO BY RAN WALKER

B-Sides and Remixes

30 Love: A Novel

Mojo's Guitar: A Novel/ (Il était une fois Morris Jones)

Afro Nerd in Love: A Novella

The Keys of My Soul: A Novel

The Race of Races: A Novel

The Illest: A Novella

Bessie, Bop, or Bach: Collected Stories

Four Floors (with Sabin Prentis)

Black Hand Side: Stories

White Pages: A Novel

She Lives in My Lap

Reverb

Work-In-Progress

Daykeeper

Most of My Heroes Don't Appear On No Stamps

Portable Black Magic: Tales of the Afro Strange

The Strange Museum: 50-Word Stories

Bees + Things + Flowers: Microfictions

The World Is Yours: Microfictions

Can I Kick It?: Sneaker Microfiction and Poetry (with Van Garrett)

The Golden Book: A 50-Year Marriage Told In 50-Word Stories

Keep It 100: 100-Word Stories

A Burst of Gray: A Novel In 100-Word Stories

The Library of Afro Curiosities: 100-Word Stories

Black Marker: A Novel in 100-Word Stories

GloKat and the Art of Timing: A Novel in 100-Word Stories

A Different Kind of Christmas Story: A Carol in 100-Word Stories

Spaceships Don't Come Equipped with Rearview Mirrors: 50-Word Stories

This Is Not a Poem/Story: 100-Word Stories

Parts of Speech: 100-Word Stories

Four Suits: 100-Word Stories